HALLOWEEN HEARTS

Also by Adele Gardner

Dwarf Stars 2022
(coedited with Greer Woodward for the
Science Fiction & Fantasy Poetry Association)

Dreaming of Days in Astophel
(as Lyn C. A. Gardner)

News of individual poems & stories through
gardnercastle.com

Also from Jackanapes Press

AVAILABLE NOW

Past the Glad and Sunlit Season: Poems for Halloween
by K. A. Opperman / Illustrated by Dan Sauer

October Ghosts and Autumn Dreams: More Poems for Halloween
by K. A. Opperman / Illustrated by Dan Sauer

The Withering: Poems of Supernatural Horror
by Ashley Dioses / Illustrated by Mutartis Boswell

The Voice of the Burning House
by John Shirley / Illustrated by Dan Sauer

The Ettinfell of Beacon Hill: Gothic Tales of Boston
by Adam Bolivar / Illustrated by Dan Sauer

Book of Shadows: Grim Tales and Gothic Fancies
by Manuel Arenas / Illustrated by Dan Sauer

The Miskatonic University Spiritualism Club
by Peter Rawlik / Illustrated by Dan Sauer

Really, Really, Really, Really Weird Stories
(A New Edition with Four New Stories) by John Shirley

The Eldritch Equations and Other Investigations
by Peter Rawlik

*Not a Princess, but (Yes) There Was a Pea and
Other Fairy Tales to Foment Revolution*
by Rebecca Buchanan

I Awaken in October: Poems of Folk Horror and Halloween
by Scott J. Couturier

COMING IN 2023

Darker Than Weird: Fourteen Tales of Horror
by John R. Fultz

www.JackanapesPress.com
www.facebook.com/Jackanapes-Press

HALLOWEEN HEARTS

ADELE GARDNER

FOREWORD BY S. T. JOSHI

JACKANAPES PRESS

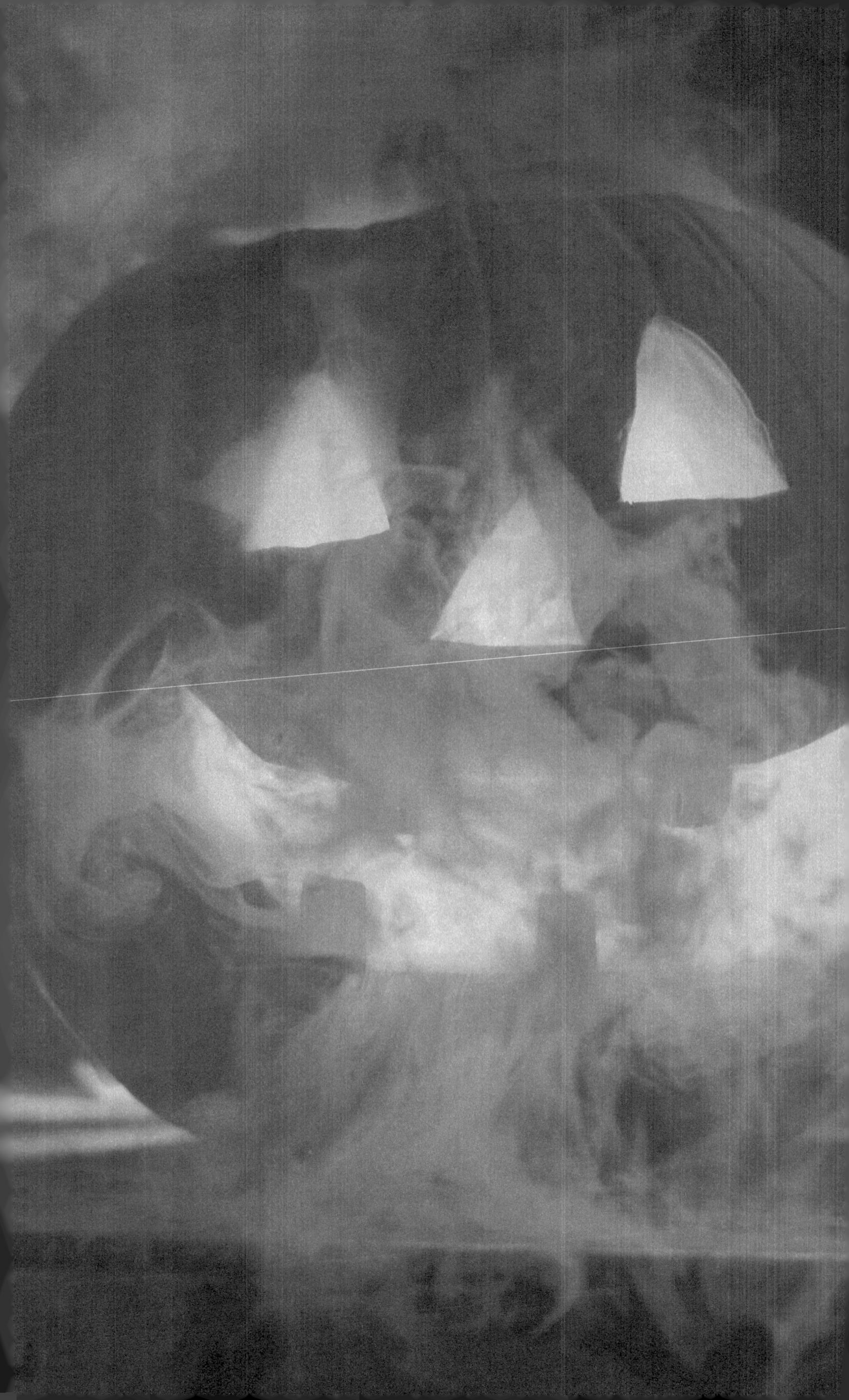

Contents

Foreword

It is remarkable how the idea of Halloween—the primitive agricultural festival of All-Hallows' Eve, dating to neolithic times and thought to be the time when witches and other night-creatures roam the earth—endures in today's cultural environment. Even if many believe it is nothing more than an occasion for children to secure toothsome candy, most people are aware that there is something sinister about the day (and night) that can inspire dread, terror, and unease. Literary figures since the eighteenth century have made extensive use of this event for conveying the deepest fears of the human race.

It is singularly appropriate that Adele Gardner has utilized the medium of poetry to convey a distinctive take on Halloween. In virtually every culture, poetry preceded prose as a medium of expression, and it is poets who have deftly adapted the age-old themes associated with Halloween and the weird in general—witches, ghosts, black cats, vampires, haunted houses—to engender horror. Adele manipulates all these motifs in a manner that resonates with today's audience, using free verse, metrical verse, acrostics, prose-poetry, and even haiku with a skill and assurance that earn our admiration.

Two writers in particular, Edgar Allan Poe and Ray Bradbury, seem closest to Adele's heart. They are wise choices. Poe's work is a seminal contribution to the literature of the weird, and his understanding of the psychology of fear was pioneering. Adele finds in Poe's life as well as his work a plangency and overriding sorrow that only enhance his horrific conceptions. Bradbury's entire career was devoted to evoking the wonders and terrors of adolescence and Halloween. In following in their footsteps, Adele Gardner does some fine evoking as well, as when we read: "I'm trapped in waking nightmares. Evil's won."

These poems are by turns chilling, ominous, poignant, and thought-provoking. They point to a poetic sensibility that can perceive the inner significance in even the simplest acts or events, and is able to use the time-tried symbols of weird literature in a way that gives them renewed potency to contemporary readers. Gardner's poems should be savored slowly, one at a time, so that their full effect can enter our consciousness. And they should be read over and over again, as each new reading will bring to light new meanings and new shades of emotion. But most of all, they inspire that "pleasing terror" which M. R. James knew is the very essence of weird writing.

—S. T. Joshi

Halloween in Our Hearts

I first met Ray Bradbury in my junior high library—in *The Halloween Tree*, the 1972 Alfred A. Knopf edition illustrated by Joseph Mugnaini, with its glowing orange title and windblown jack-o'-lantern tree.

Such wonder in that book! I renewed and read it again and again. In the long, deep blackness of those Kentucky nights, where we lived then—under the silver moon, with the call of the owl in our high trees—I drank in Ray Bradbury's perpetual ode to Halloween, his Tree carving a glowing path to the world of the spirit and the time of year I loved best.

I reverently removed the dust jacket to display both it and the library book separately on my desk. The black cloth spine bore the title stamped in Halloween orange; on the cover, a skeletal, orange mask grinned, its strings tossed on a Halloween wind. I studied the stark beauty of the pen-and-ink illustrations that brought the Night to life: the perfect, haunting complement to Bradbury's exciting prose that read like verse, his lyrical, joyful exploration of Halloween, fall and friendship, life and death.

I hunted down all the Bradbury I could find, eagerly following him to places wondrous and strange; to the October Country and Mars and Green Town, on wings built and homegrown. And I returned again to the Tree: sheer magic.

Everywhere, Bradbury's voice rang out: full of life, of joy, even when singing of death; even when trembling with grief—or terror. For Bradbury gave himself fully to every moment, every emotion, and we live with him in those moments—be they horrifying or wonderful—or both. Always, his love shines through—for life, nature, childhood, fellow beings, even the dark and the things that scare him most.

I met Ray Bradbury in person when I was twenty-four, at the Palm Springs Writers Conference; by then, I'd loved him half my life. Yet I was so shy I could barely speak to the man whose work I admired so much. Ray Bradbury, kind and gentle, talked to me through my awe and fright, and not only signed my copy of *The Halloween Tree*, but drew a grinning jack-o'-lantern inside as I told him how much I loved the book (and Halloween, and all his tales); and how it had, in many ways, started everything for me.

He shared his wisdom with us in the sessions—and his great encouragement, his optimism for us as writers, as he urged us to give in to the exuberant joy of writing. Still only a few years old at that point, Bradbury's *Zen in the Art of the Writing* remains one of the best craft books I've ever read. But for me, the most important part of the conference was those few minutes talking with him—his shy smile and his warmth as he assured me how much he still loved Halloween and what a joy it was to write that book.

That moment shines for me like a Halloween lantern in the dark night of the soul.

Speaking of such midnights dreary…

I first met Edgar Allan Poe when our sixth-grade English teacher played a record of Vincent Price reading "The Tell-Tale Heart"—electrifying! Terrifying! It still gives me chills.

I raced home to enthuse to Mom, only to discover my parents owned a complete set of black-bound volumes of Edgar Allan Poe (Collier and Sons, 1903, handed down in my mother's family with care). After some discussion, they decided to entrust me with the volumes one at a time. Each of these five black hardbacks, battered by love, bore a silver-stamped portrait of the Raven atop the bust of Pallas, along with Poe's signature and the legend, *The Works of Edgar Allan Poe*, Raven Edition. Utterly gripped, fascinated, and petrified, I hearkened to "The Bells," dwelt with "Annabel Lee," lost myself in "The Masque of the Red Death," and cowered at "The Cask of Amontillado."

Though the narrator's cruelty in "The Black Cat" proved unendurable at that young age, and I fled for a time, I reencountered Poe when we moved from Virginia to Kentucky, in English textbooks throughout junior high. The clincher came when our ninth-grade English teacher screened Vincent Price in *The Pit and the Pendulum* and Martin Landau in *The Fall of the House of Usher*. Happily, this also fell during the period when Dad and I began discussing literature more seriously, and I dove into Poe's original Usher, exploring all the cracks in this haunted house with Dad, my guide in writing and life.

During our visits to his brother in Richmond, Dad took us to the memorial marker of Poe's mother, Elizabeth Arnold Poe, in the graveyard of Historic St. John's Church and to the grave of Poe's beloved foster mother Frances Allan at the Shockoe Hill Cemetery. Later, I glimpsed Poe's grave in Baltimore on my honeymoon, and had the good fortune to "meet" Mr. Poe several times in the person of interpreters such as Richard Askew at haunted walks for the Hampton History Museum. I've appeared on several Poe panels for RavenCon, dressed as two Poe characters for Unhappy Hours at the Casemate Museum (the narrator of "Berenice") and Poe Museum (Lenore), and co-hosted two Edgar Allan Poe events at Hampton Public Library.

During one particularly hard period in my life—in which I would ultimately lose four family members to death and another to divorce within three and a half years—the Big Read came to Virginia Beach and brought Poe back into my life with a slate of library events including a poetry contest, book club, Poe-themed craft, and the chance to hear Harry Lee Poe speak about his Edgar Award-winning *Edgar Allan Poe: An Illustrated Companion to His*

Tell-Tale Stories. Crushed by grief, I'd almost stopped writing, but my beloved Poe revived me—showing me with every word that he understood; his terrors spoke to my soul.

My last chance to phone my dear Aunt Jeanne came during the Big Read. I was stuck several states away, and wanted more than anything to be with her. We'd always shared a creative fire and an appreciation for the humorous and bizarre. She could understand, but words came hard for her as cancer overcame her brain. After I told her how much I appreciated and loved her, I groped for some good news to comfort her, but the only bright thing in my life was this dark spark from Poe—who'd rekindled my muse not only through the affinity of grief, but also his surprising humor (which many people forget). My witty Aunt, who could barely speak, told me with love, enthusiasm, and humor to "Write on!" These were among her last words to me.

And so, with every year, my understanding of this holiday—this Halloween state of mind—has deepened. Halloween is not just the Night for me; it's a feeling I carry all year long. It creeps up on me with the first scent of fall and the thrill of new beginnings; the love of spooky fun, but also the longing for ghosts and the dead. As Mom's Irish heritage would have it, it marks the death of one year and birth of another: the night when spirits cross the borders between this life and another world.

I've loved Halloween since I was three, when my mother first brought out her candles of ghosts and black cats on fences, her metal noisemakers with pictures of witches and owls, her cardboard jack-o'-lantern face and springy scarecrows. She gave me the choice to become anyone—then, like a witch, granted my wish and transformed me into a black cat.

But now, with a deeper understanding of loss, I also grasp the thrill of Ray Bradbury's joy in the face of death—knowing you'll lose the people you cherish, but baring your teeth at death in a ghastly grin and *enjoying* those loved ones, no matter what. Flying into that glorious night with eyes wide open, in wonder and in fear.

From age six when I sat with Mom in our kitchen in upstate New York, drawing pictures and writing stories for my first Halloween book; to my first forays into poetry at age nine with a series of Halloween haiku; this book has been a long time coming, with its black cats and witches, ghosts and the grave, vampires and writers that haunt the night. Whether their subjects are traditional to Halloween or on tangential themes, all these poems are Halloween to me—that season so melancholy and elegiac, yet also fierce, with shining teeth, pointy grins, and a cat's fang-filled mischief.

Speaking of cats, I would like to thank Max, my Halloween cat and muse, who inspired many of these poems; who sat with me while I wrote many others; and to whom I read this book aloud several times during our final October days together. It seems no coincidence to me that both Bradbury and Poe also loved black cats.

And now, let us bask in the night, the unexplained, the mystery and magic of Halloween, which invites us to both hide and reveal our true selves—a night of contradictions; the fright that cheers.

May you carry Halloween in your hearts with joy.

—Spookily Yours,
Adele Gardner

Halloween Hearts
(for Ray Bradbury)

The master of Halloween
sets his secrets in a row:
jars and phials and demons' fangs
perched close to edges on high shelves,
ready to leap into the master's head.
Puppeteer, he builds his scene so wide
he disappears inside with just a trace
of howling in the wind, a signature of dust
as ephemeral and yet ubiquitous as grace,
hoofprints and feather-brushes mingled
till the chill autumn rain washes them away.
His mind aflame with fevered Halloween dreams,
the big orange moon rising high
to turn the carnival grounds to the ridges of a red planet,
the Ferris wheel spinning screamers up to the moon—
the cars come back down again, empty
save for shadows. Fertile with the skittering
life of flaming red and orange leaves, the master's pen
blooms Halloween hearts: grotesque, twisted, scarcely human,
the electric and eternal:
black cats, grandmothers bionic or dead,
and yet sometimes more alive than we.
Tattooed, jar-kept, electrified:
the Halloween tree jangles the ornaments of their flesh
(all flesh is grass) and sings of all our lives:
the odd and strange, the lonely and ignored:
but also the loved and not-yet-lost, the perfect, joyous childhood,
the haunts and pranks and magic and wonder
behind every bush and cellar door, never quite gone,

just rolled up and tucked dry and safe in
the hollow behind our withered, preserved hearts.
He takes them out, odd puppets from their box,
shakes out the strings, sets them to dance:
new life! new air! Lifted to Mars, the moon, the
stars, the skeletal heights of this Halloween tree,
sketched out in pen-and-ink,
penned Halloween magic.

Joy-filled boy-at-heart, this master of the dark,
brimful of the song of life and night,
the gasping wonder of it, sees with a child's fresh eyes
even when the sights are bitter.
Can't sit still, have to run out and do, do, do!
We must live again, live forever!
—even if we tumble into the ravine by night
to break our necks. We're dazzled by sparks
from the flaming leaves of truth
writ large as the sky and space, these fiery stars
of orange and red, brown and black,
fluttering like charred pages,
the richness and color of a life—
and don't forget that silver whisper
of robots and the dead. In his devil's workshop
where he plays (not works) with glee,
the billion names of God are bottled
for him to discover and release
one by one, blossoming, unfolding like paper flowers,
burning lanterns, or cut-sponge secrets,

homunculi pushing out from the chrysalis
to bloom into full-blown men or crinkle-eyed little boys
sparkling with mischief, wonder, love—
or ignored old women with entire worlds in their gnarled hearts,
compressed and rich as a dusty Martian landscape
to which a soul-flying young girl can return.
How many times has this tree bloomed,
full of deep soul-frights and skull-sweet treats,
an eye-opener that knocks your socks off,
never flinching from joy that explodes the mind
with stars or digs despair deeper than a grave,
soft, pungent earth, pity and sympathy,
terror and delight—embracing the strange,
the twisted, finding corpse-flower beauty
even through the fright? This dark carnival,
Halloween night, this Halloween life through the ages,
this day of dark and (de)light, celebrated
by so many in different disguises around the world:
with our Halloween hearts in our Halloween treetops,
across his Halloween moon, we howl to the universe:
Ray Bradbury is the cat's pajamas.

The Witch Girl

The witch girl crouches beside her cauldron,
chain dragging from an iron collar like a dog's.
They don't trust her yet with the bones they grind
to make their soup. They caught her gnawing, snarfing down
her own leg in the woods, starvation slimming her throat
so the bones of her ankle caught in her craw,
choking they mistook for a witch-chick's first attempt to cackle.

Now she stirs broth, the base for spells:
plastic filters from a forest fire; shards of shattered star;
Sweet William three days dead, the flesh
still succulent on his bones. He'd been rotting,
dropping pieces of himself, a dirty white trail of breadcrumbs
that the vultures and hyenas loved. The witch girl followed,
collecting him in her basket, popping his leavings in her mouth
till flesh melted from bones, sweet with his charm that won every heart.
Mother, our caravan queen, always loved him best—
she mixes his *memento mori* in every spell, small bones to remind us
of him with their delicate crunch, perhaps with a strand woven in
of those fine golden locks she doles out one by one,
keeping the rest to build the girl a husband when the time comes.

Right now the girl is barely more than feral—
fruitless to comb that storm-cloud hair or trim it with bones,
though tinsel might be nice, if any shards of broken star are left.
She's got to look frightful in case the town creeps by for thrills.
But the wild gleam in her swamp-dark eyes may be enough.
She pins you with that stare, animal malice, human deceit,
the scorn of a dirty trick, the first prick of capture
before the killing jar.

When the witches roll into town, setting up wagons under the trees,
guarded by a fence of crossed broomsticks—beware.
The witch girl lures you in, skinny child needing solace,
her gaunt, dirty cheeks aiding her pleas for staples:
An eye, perhaps? You have a spare. That great big nose? Whittle off
a few ounces. Your brain? You won't miss it. Fingers make
delicious finger-food. She's so cute, ragamuffin waif—you pity her, forget
she's already a witch at heart. Fire glares orange through the moon-cut door
behind which her sisters beckon, luring unwary rest-stop seekers
to add their exotic, well-traveled flavors to the soup.
If you're lucky, the witch girl will honor you by stretching your tattoos
from two crossed poles to catch the wind, Halloween banner
under the moon, strong scent to distract the townies till she bangs her pot
with that menacing glare: You next. They scamper.

She's more than wolf-bred—more like the slough of self-deceit,
mother-hatred, self-loathing, repudiated love, the bitter strength
of a heart turned sour, a putrid and terrifying drink.
The witch girl smites you with that killing stare,
the frank malice of her scowl, the dark night where her soul lurks.
Her tangled hair and dirt-smeared face, her bloody rags
where limbs poke through like bones, might incite sympathy
if she didn't hate you all so fiercely. It's intriguing, the way she stirs
that pot of dashed hopes with her ladle of bone. Is that your leg?

After all, you haven't come home. You cursed me last night,
before you stormed out without your keys: you'd go to the caravan
to seek your fortune—find yourself. You wouldn't wait for an umbrella,
just ran out into the sleet, yelling that it wasn't me, and what was there
to leave behind? Your defiant look so much like hers—those black eyes
full of hate. That heart-bloody sleeve. That patch of bright, gnawed bone
where you chewed yourself free of this trap, to hobble into the killing wood,
leaving me here, like the witch girl, to simmer and stew
the poison that teaches me to be glad you're gone.

Haunt Me

Simka says your ghost visits her
and Sydney regularly. Why not me?
Where were you when I brushed aside
this veil of my life for one clear moment,
dreading not death, but no reunion?
Fear is the prophecy, and what
others shun I embrace: frights
both actual and metaphysical,
not for the shock, but to remind me
what you felt at the end—and perhaps through danger
call you, if you're still close enough to hear me—
if you still care. I have my doubts.
I've replaced you now three times with other men:
got a glimmer of fright with the first's drunken car wreck;
a frisson of fear as the second lost his job due to a fire
on our one-year anniversary;
but so far nothing but nightmares with the third,
which he claims are normal for his level of insomnia,
though he doesn't understand
why a skinny redhead with a broken nose
keeps chasing him with a hatchet.
If this is prophecy, I'm touched you care.
But I long for you in my dreams, and languish
here alone, waiting for some last sign
now that I've sent this latest love away:
should I drain my kettle and join you?
Or is hell too far to carry a torch?

Home Inspection

Each time we move
I consult my local ghost appraiser:
Spirits Local 13—
plenty of good mediums for the right price
to come in, sense disturbances and disruptions,
Find the fractures,
send out a line to discover how far they go
and what exists on the other side.

I love a beautiful old Victorian;
love best to imagine the lives
of those who enjoyed a house before me—
nooks where they read,
staircases where they slid,
balconies where they played,
those secret passages
(and what the secrets were).

But who wants to sleep
in the chilliest room
not knowing if you'll hear the secrets of life
whispered in your ear,
or be sucked by a hungry ghost
into an early grave?

Even though the medium says all's clear,
I wish I'd required
a sleepover in the contract,
to see how quiet the house is by night.
I wake by pallid moonlight
to see a little girl in gingham
at the foot of my four-poster
(so large I need a set of stairs
like the ghosts of my cats).
Her ornate ruffles and bows
make the ragged length of her locks
look like patchwork
as she holds out a hair-wreath,
her blue lips mouthing the words,
"For you."

Witch Habiliments

Witches who fly by country night
wear black by dark of moon.
Some spangle themselves with stars,
whole constellations mapped in zirconia
or glow-in-the-dark polka dots.
Purple suits a city night, metro-trim,
suburban midnight washed out
even without the moon. By daylight,
the poorer witches dress like twigs,
knobby wrists and knees wrapped up in sackcloth
rough as bark, their brittle, flyaway brown hair
blending them into branches,
hidden by the trees who gladly lend dry sticks
for the bundles of crooked brooms.
In spring, some stitch new sprigs of green and blue,
drape themselves in diaphanous pink and white
as they sail through sunset clouds.
Beware of witches camped in nudist colonies,
their hook noses and scraggly hair
hidden perfectly in a forest of others,
nakedness more invisible than a spell.
But Halloween's their favorite:
that's when witches don their finery,
hair dyed red as flaming leaves,
dresses layered in jagged orange and rich brown
for prowling through harvest fields,
deep red and black to beat the devil
and set the match to bonfires
in the dark nights of the soul.

Camouflaged in nightmares,
they cackle through your dreams.
On Halloween night, flying before the moon,
they edge the dark of the blackest night
with trim that shines
with captured hearts of gold.

Black Cat Spare

I always have a black cat handy—
Here, you need a spare?
Don't think we witches have life easy—
Bad luck cast is shared.

The Chant of the Black Cats

We are Halloween: we black cats,
puddles that vanish into night,
our green eyes flashing like horizon light
that warns of ships that drowned
because no good-luck black cats
prowled the decks, fending off storms,
brushing sailors with midnight magic.
As Halloween cats, we keep watch
behind curtains, atop fences, underneath cars.
It's our night, and we lash our tails, puff wide,
fill hollows so deep we're only floating eyes.
A Halloween moon's best, harvest orange,
fat as a pumpkin, a gleam as sweet as pies.
We braid it into whisker-threads, weave mystic light
in a paw-dance across the path of those who need our luck.

We march in sleek black funeral attire,
a slinky but precise procession:
every step counts, spells widdershins,
ace in the hole and a paw to keep it there.
Inspired by us, you parade your young
like a lioness showing her cubs to the pride,
your own kittens wrapped in flamboyant pelts,
nudged to walk on their own to ring the bell,
present themselves, say the magic words,
a regal procession rich with ritual
that unifies you for a single night,
even the babes in arms brought close for approval,
while proud parents stand back, watching
the cubs play at hunting treats on their own.

It's the most dangerous night of the year.
Roads are always bad, but Halloween turns black cats
from hunters into prey. Tin cans and tail-burnings,
E. A. Poe hangings, living burials. House cats get trussed
in fancy clothes, protesting with ululating yowls,
distracted from their mission: to spot spirits that slide through cracks,
rousting them like rodents, vigilant to preserve
the warmth of the home, while the hard months begin outside—
frost, starvation, as mice hibernate and birds fly south—
No food banks for cats, and shelters overflow,
spelling more feline deaths.

Despite the need for our Halloween magic,
we've had to give up perching on fence posts
in orderly, obvious rows. Now we cluster
in skeletal trees where you can't get us—
wary of owls, our claws sunk deep in bark
to keep from being snatched and flown away
while above us, great horned owls chuckle:
We'll eat you, black cats, they hoot
while we hunker in the crooks of branches.

We peer down with the luster of ambers and greens,
the menacing sparkle of Halloween lights.
Velvet brushes your cheek—cold rush as our tails anoint you
with Halloween magic, the chill finger of death
to keep you on your toes. You duck and scream,
run, fleet, young again as we shiver you alive
with electric fur and fine, needle-prick claws,
slipping through night to thread our nine lives through yours
like stitches, binding the rents in your spirit,
Frankenstein's monster stitched whole and new,
pumped full of lightning, galvanized by fear.

Midnight Posture

This midnight posture cramps the back.
Time was my black cat jumped into my lap, climbed up my chest,
Slipped across shoulders to drape his tail around my neck,
Tail tickling my chin. I tilted forward, carrying him,
Balancing his weight against my neck while he draped my shoulders,
Bending forward when he slipped till he curled solid on my back,
And I walked hunched like a shelf not to dislodge him.
He purred and I rested
Across the back of the loveseat,
Elbows propped to watch TV while he settled in a sprawl,
Rumbling long after the rest of him slowed in sleep
Like a ghost lingering behind.
Now, several deaths later, I rise from my chair
With a weight huddled high on my chest
Till it claws its way up to press, familiar,
Against my neck, slipping down at last to settle on my back,
Bowing me under each night I prowl,
Unable to sleep under the weight of dreams,
Of father, uncles, grandmother suffering, sinking into death,
Me helpless, paralyzed, to save them.
My midnight crossing: I carry my own dead
Everywhere I go, pilgrim with a burden,
All I can do: never to let them go.
I'll balance till I'm on my knees
Rather than let one ghost fall.

My Little Vampire

Gabrielle loved vampires, and she
thought she might have found one.
He weighed fourteen pounds
and was covered with black fur,
had a squeaky little meow,
and answered to the name of Max.
She knew vampires
sometimes roamed the night
in the form of bats, wolves,
or black cats. Night after night,
Max stood outside her
bedroom door, crying to get in.
When Gabrielle opened the
door, he still stood there,
pleading, clearly wanting to join
her, putting one cautious foot
forward, then pulling it back
as if the threshold was
an impassible barrier. Each night,
she invited him inside.

Pandemic Food Delivery

Far from native soil,
barred by travel bans, greedy
for fruits from that earth

Gone the Sun

night draping black across my eyes,
hurrying the sunset
into the deathly silence of
vampire folds:
gone now,
the burning danger of
the sun-blaze of your love

Our Last Halloween

For our last Halloween
we wore cat masks,
thin cardboard cut
from a catfood giveaway
tied on with string.
Your sad dark eyes
looked out at me, mismatched
through kid-size holes.
Maybe your cold kept you subdued.
You baked small Halloween drop cookies
the size of silver dollars or Easter money
with chocolate black cats in the middle.
Our cats chased Halloween toys:
a mini-pumpkin, Frankenstein's hairy eyeball,
little catnip puffs of ghosts and werewolves
they greedily snapped up
and carried in their mouths, protecting us
from evil—including ourselves.
No fights that night as we watched Garfield,
fielded five cats, toasted each other
with witches' brews, ate pumpkin-painted donuts,
and gave each other Halloween treats:
a cloth basket like a black cat's head,
marshmallow ghosts, a puppet raven,
your favorite peanut butter sweets in orange wrappings,
but best of all
the tussle-rumbling and scary-loud purrs
of big boy catnipped cats
pouncing on the goblins
tethered at the ends of our strings.

Seven Steps to Reach Your Father across the Great Divide

1. Eat and drink enough to keep body and soul together. Important: force yourself to eat if you have to, at least a piece of bread once a day. Try to avoid stuffing everything possible in your mouth without tasting or chewing when you finally do break down and eat every few days. Try to survive on one apple a day, a little water. After a while you'll begin to float away. But watch out for the line: you still need to carry on for him, to complete his affairs, all those manuscripts to publish, and if you step too far, that big black line will grow deep as a pit and separate you forever.

2. Read books and listen to phonograph records you loved as a child, particularly those you associate with him. Sing songs he loved to sing. Immerse yourself in his laugh, his voice, his gentleness, the confiding way he'd tell you stories in the rocking chair before bed, to the sound of wind in the trees.

3. Sleep on a blanket on the floor. You can't sleep anyway, and whenever you wake your heart stops, as it hits you again: his death. The hospital. Those labored breaths. You're so cold. You hoped so much, right up until the end, and in your dreams he's suffering still, but there's some chance he'll survive. Even a few more hours would mean the world. You're crushed to the ground anyway, so the asceticism of a humble floor-bed suits your mood, your self-recriminations. There could never be enough time, but surely there were other things you could have given up to spend more with him. Now the hard floor, wedged in between the bathroom and the end of the bed and two bookshelves, with the bathroom light on all night so you don't freak out, so you'll be grounded when you wake up, remembering where you are—it's oddly comforting, as if this narrow space to curl into, on the blanket, were the treat of sleeping at the foot of your parents' bed when company comes.

4. Don't let this pain get away. Cling to it with both hands, because every
    day will carry you a step further from Dad. You can't eat. You can't sleep.
    You can't read. You can't write. There's no one to talk to—no one who
    understands but your family, who have burdens enough. Talking to
    friends is like treading on blazing rocks over an endless sea. No safe
    subject; if they don't say something, you hate them; if they do, they make
    it worse. You're only halfway through your life (how will you bear that
    second half without him?), and you're already forgetting, things slipping
    past you like the black cat who mysteriously leaps on the bed after you
    thought you left him in the hall. He can have the bed. He can have
    everything. Make a new will. Leave everything to your cats. Don't forget
    to appoint a new literary executor for Dad's work. The farther away you
    get from everyone else, the closer you get to him, the more you can hear
    him: his voice in your ear, answering your questions, your grief; when
    the grief drowns him out, only the sound of his weeping because you
    won't eat. He stopped you once before, when your fiancé left: a blow
    that felt like death at the time. Dad stood crying in the door—"I just
    want you to know how much I love you, honey. I don't want to lose
    you"—straddling the threshold to block the way to death. He stands
    there still. You can't do anything to hurt him. You only want to lie beside
    him—you picked your blue coffin the day the family chose his. You need
    to know: does hell meet the suicide, or only a father's loving arms to stop
    the pain?

5. Read his manuscripts over. Typing or proofing them, you hear his voice,
    fresh and strong and deep as it was before the lung operation. Keep
    working on his literary project even when you can hardly see for tears,
    when you groan and call for Daddy, when there's no answer except these
    words on the page, except this little slip of notepaper in his trembling
    handwriting slipped inside a conference folder—a conference you

attended together, the draft a poem about you, about a child growing into a woman and fellow poet—silently writing about you, his love for you strong as you sat right next to him in the poetry workshop, unknowing. Now he touches your hand softly. Here's an article he saved about a young MD who returned after being legally dead for thirty minutes— his wandering journey through time and space, seeing things he'd never known that later proved real. Hold onto the hope that these are messages—Dad's voice from beyond the grave.

6. Be open to signs. Watch every movie and show that proves the existence of spirits, the unexplained. Even the evil or creepy ones don't scare you now. There's nothing worse than what's already happened, and even zombies prove there's something on the other side. That the spirit remains. That the light that left his eyes didn't die, just migrated somewhere else. Maybe into your head. His last instructions concluded, "Be kind to each other. Love never dies! God bless you all!" This is the truth you pursue now in dreams—some hint, some message, the last few minutes wound back to the time he was still there. Time for all the words unsaid, the things undone—the plans you two made. Awake, you watch the shows you loved together, just for the hint he sits beside you. You can still hear him laugh. Sometimes you eat then, and you feel he's happy, that he approves. He's exerting all a spirit's energy to keep you grounded, to keep you whole, to keep you from floating away after him. Blocking the doorway yet again.

7. If all else fails, drive dangerously. Howling tears after one too many sympathetic words, you can't see the road, and the only thread holding you together is the wish not to extinguish another life. You might hit the guard rail solo through this wall of tears. You can't lose: either you'll fly across the divided highway to join him, or he'll rush back to take the

wheel. How loud must you scream for him to hear? "I'm here all along," the words pop into your head, clear, strong: his voice, so certain, that solid presence you've felt since he died, beyond the need for faith. Even while he was alive you felt his presence beside you, his smile, his cheerful comments, while you wrote alone in tribute to your mentor or watched shows you both enjoyed. Did he feel you near when you thought of him? Do linked souls share each other's spaces while still living? No one on earth loves you that much now, unquestionable, vast; no one's that happy to see you, has that much time for you. Your brother says there's a special bond between father and firstborn daughter, and God, you hope it's true. You pray for an unbreakable golden cord, a musical string stretching as long as need be to reach the places you can't see except in dreams. Dad's every day was a living promise that love never lets go. So don't forget. Hold on. Daddy loves you.

Daddy, where are you?

Home
(after "Alone" by Edgar Allan Poe)

From Dad's last breath I've wandered, ghost
In my own life—his eyes, the most
I manifest—the cord to heart
Snapped clean, I float above the chart
Of flattened life, topography
Of love reduced—I am not free
To grieve—my thread drags in the dust—
Gold Ariadne changed to rust.
Untethered, numb, lightheaded, cold—
I drift through drizzle, forfeit soul
To tramp through hell in bloody boots—
To squat in dirt, chew bitter roots
Pulled from the grave where Daddy lies,
His suit as blue as autumn skies.
We feared the flood, laid him to rest
In double vault, love-note at breast,
Eyes shut, horn-rimmed, a rose still tart
In frozen hands stiff as my heart—
Sealed tight against eternity—
But with no doorway left for me
To climb back in where Daddy lies,
My only home beneath the skies.

Eureka

*(an homage to Edgar Allan Poe and his prose
poem on the nature of the universe)*

Each time I read your work aloud, or sit listening in the
Dark, your spirit touches me: a slight pressure on the back of the neck, a
Gliding hand reaching into mine. You enter the room so softly
All thought ceases, but the rhythm of your "unified effect"
Roars through my blood: my matter vibrating in a harmony

As dangerous as the glass armonica, distorting senses, grinding nerves thin
Like the nervous sensibility of all your heroes. No
Liquid could carry sound more cunningly than your words, breathing your
    living voice.
Awareness deepens of each heartbeat in the room, each rising chorus—
No, I dare not listen! Your distemper batters at my brain,

Pulling me farther into your dark heart till I must burst
Or go mad! Where are you? Where? I turn and you are
Everywhere, everything—all souls shared, *Eureka*—my bones are yours!

A Keepsake Box for Poe

(Quotes are from "The Tell-Tale Heart" by Edgar Allan Poe)

Your grave transplanted in effigy
to this library bicentennial celebration
of your birth, your books decorated by
branches of ravens and black leaves,
cast-iron fence and roses,
Gothic's horrific, beatific emphasis
on the sublime: your papier-mâché headstone
a marker to a storm cellar of the mind
where we can all escape
the ravages of time:
January 19, 1809–October 7, 1849—
too short a span for us to grasp,
but immaterial to one
whose words still breathe
on our lips and echo in our minds:
"I heard all things in the heaven and in the earth.
I heard many things in hell.
How, then, am I mad?"

Curled up in the edges, these scraps
will save us: lost thoughts, lost minutes,
the clock ticking falsely, a phony heartbeat
that drums life away,
but only if we believe it can.
In the meantime, we subsist
on stolen moments, the fragments you left,
your meaning a message from beyond the grave:
"It was a low, dull, quick sound—
much such a sound as a watch makes
when enveloped in cotton."

We find unconscious reference points
in this perceived fixation with the human eye:
eyes everywhere, decorating the trees, your grave,
one staring eye reflected—
"the eye of a vulture—
a pale blue eye, with a film over it"
in a pond where your image lies
face up to the reflection of the moon.

We wanted answers: pried you loose,
rattled your bones, shook your skeletal hands
till only dust remained. Still, we'll never know
the secret name of your raven,
pet the reincarnation of your black cat,
or discover where you hid your heart so many years ago,
under the floorboards
of your beloved's coffin,
safe from love and death,
from time—
from us.
"Presently I heard a slight groan—
the low stifled sound that arises
from the bottom of the soul
when overcharged with awe."

Poe's Prophets

One raven flying,
two ravens crouching on a branch,
three ravens cawing rough talk across stormy skies,
those wicked eyes hanging innocent from their twigs
amongst burnt black leaves—staring back from forever,
from this pit where Edgar languishes and writhes
while we perpetuate his horrors, feed his legend,
give him nightmares
lo these many years
since his "Nevermore" first winged
into our minds,
ravens flying, perching, haunting
every last one of us.

Nevermore

No one now living knows the truth—
Edgar, your mysterious death haunts me
Vigorously, as relentless as Montresor
Entombing his former friend.
Revenge for your Raven or your many loves?
Murder as vile as your tales, your character assassinated
Only too well by Griswold—vile as your worst villains.
Ravens roost on your grave, carrying messages to
Everyone you ever loved.

Lenore to Her Tragic Muse, Edgar Allan Poe

(Jan. 19, 1809-Oct. 7, 1849)
In Answer to His Own "The Raven"

Once within the drear October, days I scarcely dare remember,
Still believing that the faith of one could conquer fatal woe,
Messenger arrived most evil, letter penned by drink or devil,
News about my love primeval, dead forever—Edgar Poe!
Alas, my tragic, lost, forlorn, beloved Edgar Allan Poe!
      Yowled the black cat, "Let him go!"

How might maiden part the curtain, slip behind to view his burden,
Find the secret source of hurt that answered happiness with "No"?
And how live with this dark mischief, cat as black as Satan's kerchief,
Bringing me the word I purchased without heed for cost or woe—
My lover's heart, subsumed by grief for one he loved, now ash and woe—
      Yowled the black cat, "Let him go!"

Still I hung, dazed maiden martyr—with each tug clung tighter, harder,
To that rope which deep into the awful Stygian grave did go—
"Love," I gasped, "let loose the curtain—show your heart, howe'er uncertain—
Take me not into the grave by way of parcelling your woe—
From this grim portion spare the maid who unto death doth love you so—"
      Yowled the black cat, "Let him go!"

Then I spied stones cast asunder, crumbled by some deadly thunder,
As though grief propelled the sleeper to cast off the name of Poe—
Step out of the tomb that carried ghosts of all the loved and buried,
Mother, bride, his own name storied, world-renowned Edgar A. Poe—
How I pined for my own lost and tragic Edgar Allan Poe—
      Yowled the black cat, "Let him go!"

In a dream that stole my senses, dark as Edgar's hair and lenses
Of his soul, those dearest eyes that ever let love's true tears flow,
So he wept for wife and mother—so weep I, 'fianced no longer,
To that tender soul whose squandered secrets went to grave below,
Heart so tender there to fester in that self-dug grave below—
                        Yowled the black cat, "Let him go!"

"No!" I cried. "I love forever! Spin me out no tales of censure,
Stories of the ladies swooning to the voice of Edgar Poe,
Still declaiming, still declaiming, in his ringing voice, that Raven
Who rends still my heart—with claws now, in his cat-shape, sly and low,
A witchy, slinky shape of omen, growls sepulchral, hollow—No!"
                        Yowled the black cat, "Let him go!"

"I cannot! I shall haunt eternal that lost heart, to keep it vernal!
Poe lives on in me, e'en should his shade have nowhere else to go!"
But the black cat chuckled, prowling, with scoring claws, unearthly yowling,
Demanded I pay heed to one foul note I'd rather burn than know:
Words my pining lover wrote when of my breath he did not know—
                        Die not for me, my Edgar Poe!

To Hear You Speak

There's nothing that might move me much
    Except to hear you speak:
My lover of the cloven wings
    And of the silver beak.

What poetry would sprout to life,
    True to your graceful breed,
Each word a pearl from rainbow spout,
    Each epigram, a creed?

Who might resist the wise, succinct,
    And pointed words, as sharp
As feather's steel or roseblood claw,
    Lodged delicate in my heart?

Since inspiration from your kind
    First struck us, true and whole,
The human blood drawn in your quill
    Ecstatic, to the soul—

I've trembled, quivering for the day
    You'll pipe to me alone—
Pin me with sly and speaking eye
    And pluck me to the bone.

Late

5 A.M.
I never get over the panic as the lid swings shut,
those last few minutes before the sun rises,
trying to hold my arms down by my sides until I'm
trembling all over, until my hands
rise of their own accord
to pound against white velvet, long since in tatters,
a new nail
piercing the flesh of my fist
as my body explodes in a frenzy of
pounding
and clawing
worse than any scream,
seconds before I am to sleep.
I wake that way, stiff and straining,
eyes dry and bulging as a victim of
rigor mortis.
You can't tell me it's
simple
as lying down for the night,
amidst smooth white satin sheets.
Every night when they lock us in the crypt—
for our own protection—
my heart shatters with panic.
A helplessness that links me to them yet,
beyond all other changes,
a reflex beyond mortality or time,
a mortal reflex.
They are burying
me alive.

Morning, for me, is not what you might expect.
My day does not begin
when all your lamps are lit,
when you sit back comfortably in the gloom
to scare yourself with stories.
Your day is my day.
Your sun, the one I still ache for
like a lover.
I never slept well
even while dreaming my way
through a mortal life,
and now I feel the subtle shifts in clouds,
in leaves and branches,
as the sun passes overhead,
imagine the sun on my skin
like a plant that lusts
to drink this golden nectar.
Night
is only that—my night.
It is always very late.

I am always about to die.

I Wander in the Mists

*(after Gerard Manley Hopkins's
"[I Wake and Feel the Fell of Dark, Not Day]")*

I wander in the mists of sleep, not sight.
What waking, startled hour, brought this wood,
This fog! What straining, eyes, you tried; squinting withstood!
And sightless still, bound far from freedom, light.
In dread I tell. For I slept not that night,
But drifted past hope, past haven. My only food
Stores sickness, a sweet to choke the soul with good
Now gall, stale flesh's fine, ah! fled delight.

I am blind, I am burning. Eyes that stole too much
Now dim past darkening: seared from forbidden touch;
Hands held too long, fingers falter, nails black with sun.

Brightness too vivid soon washes down dim. Love such
That I desired most, deserts my clutch
Like memory's fog, blinding all sights; save one.

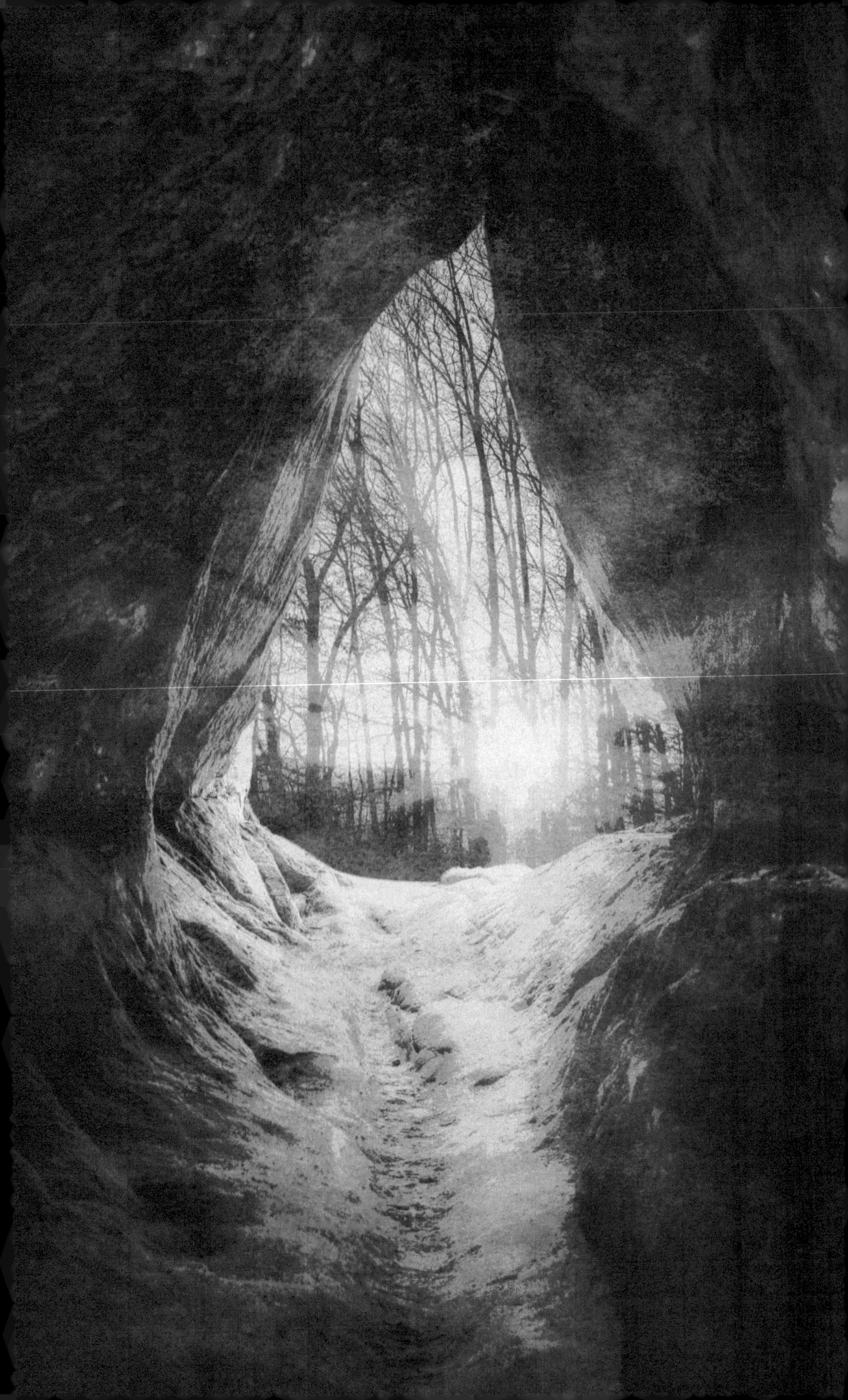

Golden Eye

The sun, that winking golden eye,
mocked my childish yearning for its face.
I stretched starfish hands,
small pudgy fingers groping for an amber ball,
that perfect sphere straight out of ancient children's books
where all the kids are happy—fool's gold.
The guardians in that cold house warned me,
"You must not look lest you go blind."
But I tricked it out of mirrors,
practiced quick glimpses, seared bronze behind my eyes.
Comforting as my imagined mother's touch,
my stolen sun, ephemeral yet ever-present,
a smile that shared secrets, a best friend's wink,
celestial warmth for one who had no family, no friends,
the odd child whistling as she walked home
in afternoon's shower of intangible gold.

For some, dreams die with childhood:
in that void, the darkness rushes in,
even before our mortal span is up,
this human shell cracked open to endless night.
Already sunny life spills out our ears,
trickling free like sawdust from a doll
whose seams erode with age as she forgets
the tight-laced boundaries that marked her shape in the world.
All those adult voices, cajoling me:
"That sun can't speak. It's immature to talk
to an imaginary friend." That sun, whose booming voice
had filled my days with light and fire, whittled down
to a wood-knuckle, just a flat disc in the sky.

Gone, my warm and rumbling friend,
the speaking sun dimmed with the years,
fading into a sorrow I had no name for,
as I worked late into the night. Gone, that chuckle
that surprised me with its sudden glint of gold on water,
on a leaf, red through my hand,
my snuck glimpse of a wry eye that knew my name.
Gone, that little fool who believed
she felt his actual touch upon her shoulder,
warm fingers spreading like a father's hand;
who thought that a giant sun could speak—
and if it could, that it would talk to her.
Grown wise, I spend my days working inside
in a windowless room, caved in with the melancholy
of a distant, private life, locked up safe.

But when I close my eyes, I still see that burning ball:
it rolls on ahead, a perfect, golden sphere,
dwindling, distant, a pinprick, gone.
I'm not quick or brave enough to seize
its offered comfort. I feel my way in the dark, in a maze,
fumbling to light a candle in these damp caverns.
At last I catch up to a glint that looks like hope,
but it's so dim—I press it to my lips,
longing for that bright, searing tang,
but taste only nectar, seductive, sweet,
forbidden as the flesh that rejected me at birth.
Trapped in these echoing tunnels, I can't hear
the sun's steady, reassuring hum,
only some soprano's torch song in a foreign tongue.

The melody leads me deeper. I'm muffled in darkness,
choked in a veiled, dusty embrace, my fingers clawing cerements,
my nostrils clogged with sawdust as if a taxidermist's stitches burst,
the cat it sealed faded past the sharp surge of separate life.
She's found me at last: my shadow-mother,
wrapping me tight in the knowledge that I am nothing—
a mistake, the wreck of her life—living death.

Beyond the reach of my golden protector,
the cave's heart swallows me.
She seizes me in an embrace that is, in the end,
not monstrous but lonely. She says I'll never leave her,
and that this taste of brimstone is the sun I seek,
burning, a nectar honeysuckle-sweet.
She draws me into an embrace scented seductively of amber,
as she presses my hands to skinned-back lips: her rigid smile.
Now I who loved the sun can't quench this thirst,
gasping and gulping a flavor rich
with the life I've left behind.
In each vein, I taste the sun, that warmth,
A miniature shining eye,
Memory of a friend I can never see again—
long vanished, a fool's hope,
a child's lost golden ball.

The Cost

You wake beside me, somnolent and slow,
The glint of morn reflected in your eyes,
The only way I see it now. Surprise
Has long since crawled to die and birth despair.
And yet you're lovelier by moonlight, guise
Of angels with your web of silver hair,
The calm of smooth-faced goddesses who bear
One's pain with ease, delight to drink one's woe.

But what if Truth opposes what I dream?
What if your eyes shine not with love, but fear—
Your heart not still, at peace, past mortal care,
But trembling, trapped, a statue broken, bare,
The marble stripped of ribbons, cracked with wear—
Immortal life dulled gray, but for the gleam
Of crimson lips and eyes that plead? We're lost,
Beyond all hope, all time—our mortal cost.

Reynardine

rug shag green
rough beneath my legs
chill of the marble
fireplace
black tiles
freezing my maiden knee

Rey sits above me
leaning back into the cushions
foot angling above knee
grayed socks on the green
lips pressed hard eyes
glinting behind glass

opens lips
teeth fox-pointed,
darts the tongue
with snake's cruel intent:
I shrivel before his
venom-barbed words

wandering innocent,
my first steps in the dark woods
of the adult world
brought me here, to a stranger
who acted kind
until he had me
safe inside

Rey said he was a soldier
like my hero father
lured me with false sympathy
now sits with gun propped on knee
pointed at my head
shows me pictures he's drawn
of girls' heads blown off

Rey says he'll let me go
if I bring him my baby sister
who will be 16 in three days
no escape but one:
I bind him to me instead
by giving up my maidenhead
on Sissy's birthday
though the pain splits me in two

for six months I labor
reduced to char-girl, body-servant
a maid no more, yet always a maid
never a bride
I will not say yes
for yes means death
if you wed Reynardine

but if you are a clever girl
you whistle as you go
to cover that one extra clink
when you get to
clean the knives

The Catty Hours

Midnight with my little black cat
Waiting for Halloween
Pricking me with his fine needle claws—
Signs of love as he purrs, purrs—
Sharp as his green eyes
Staring deep into my soul,
His pointed ears, pointed tail
Little black magic cat
Riding on my chest like the flat of a broom
As I soar through dreamland,
Guarding me,
Hissing my demons away
As anxieties dig deep
In the wee small hours
The witching hours
The canny, green-eyed hours
The catty hours
Calm dark waters, dipping cool hands
Smooth as the black velvet of midnight
(With my little black cat)
Fingers stir through purring black fur
As I smooth angled cheeks and triangle chin
That slant like his wise, glowing cat-eyes.
Max purrs me to sleep, rumbles regular as waves
Pushing me off the shore
With Wynken, Blynken, and Nod,
Sailing through star-land, dreamland,
Little black cat perched on the helm.

My long, lean, sleek and sinuous cat-man,
His tail waving like a cavalier's plume,
Honour bright as Maximilien Morrel
And his cat-like Count,
Rumbling away this tightness in my chest
That catches me, quickening my breath
To nightmares echoing this fulcrum life—
With almost as many loved ones now my beloved dead
As are still living with me on this side—
When my dead outnumber my living,
Will I dip down into that darkness?
Dip down
(into Death)
I wake to find my cheek pressed sleek
Into purring black cat fur,
And Max gazes at me
With smiling black cat eyes

A Tasty Treat

The kitchen is the best room in the house.
Not just for warmth, but precious memories—
Two grandmas baking treats and brewing spells,
My crafty decorations on the walls—
My heroes—Nimue and Morgan Faye,
And wise Italian cats who duel and scrap
And come to life at night to prowl my halls
And keep me safe from demons in the walls.
Why not live for gingerbread? I crave
The comfort of a batch already made
And waiting in the freezer for my touch
To bring a horse, boy, star, or Santa Claus
To life within my kiln with magic stuff
You can't get at the store. The children come,
As children always do, drawn by the smell,
The magic dancing ready in their eyes.
I'll bake them up a magical surprise.
The taste will bring your childhood flooding back.
It's toasty warm upon my baking rack.

Our Lady of Darkness

Send me the night, with her wide grey eyes,
Her skin white velvet, her charming lies:
Her words of heartfelt, loyal youth,
A friendship so sweet you doubt its truth:
But dare you believe, take her small, ready hand—
She'll abandon your heart in a pale, distant land.
Oh, is her grasp comforting, steady, and warm,
You'll still wake a' prayin' in the cold, gray morn.

Scorn her: you'll rush through the sun-poisoned days,
Hope dying each night with your love who betrays,
Yet like clockwork return to hell's precipice wide,
Fumbling for truth that the body must hide.
Life's fire roars urgent through translucent skin,
Through flash-paper joy, and stained-nicotine sin;
Screw the vise on the heart seeking anything firm,
For life's fluttering, uncertain, and too short to learn.

You'll wear yourself thin in Life's turbulent bed,
Limbs aching, heart breaking, each night till you're dead;
In your loneliest hour when Life spurns your groans,
She whom you cringe from will comfort your bones;
Whom you've wept for in secret, will smooth your cold feet,
Her quiet a balm, her smile gentle and sweet.
When you open your hand to her sisterly grace,
She'll take you at last to what Life would efface:
That gray, peaceful meadow, that one certain prize,
For everything dreams, and everything dies;
And she whom you feared loves you still in the end,
And you'll kiss the sweet smile of your last, best friend.

The Perfect Match

Their boughs bend low beneath her crushing hand.
(Obeisance cannot sway a grieving god.)
The living trees are helpless where they stand,
Awake and murdered by the same command.
Her scream strips leaves, breaks mountains—mad maraud
That strips the motherland to barren sod
As stark as where I shiver. Deodand
For daughter's death, when wrought by mother's plan,
Remits the hand of life to House of Death—
Where I am queen, paid in my mother's breath.
I watch, below, though soil chokes my eyes:
Demeter dooms the world for my demise—
She matched us—thought as son, Death could be bent—
But I am heir to Mother's grave intent.

Throat

My uncle stands by the sofa,
Dapper, red button-down, cocktail in hand,
Handsome with that swirl of combed-over
White hair. I'm suddenly shy:
I haven't seen him for so long.
Not since he died.
His few visits have been as thin as air:
He vanishes when I turn around,
Fades till I see right through him.
Now he cocks his jaunty hat.
I can't stop smiling. His grin says he knows why.
He's as solid now as that rock in my heart,
Wishing him home.
I hug him hard because I can't
Tell him how much I've missed him—
I don't dare risk that subject.

He doesn't fade. He mingles, drink in hand,
Red kerchief tight about his throat,
Scarlet as his blood—I don't dare ask.
He winks, unties it, the cloth cutting his hands.

Hollow. Stripped bare. He has no throat.
A strip below his head, clear to the room behind him.
He places a hand to cover what's erased,
Like a finger holding back a secret.

He takes me by the throat.
His grip, so solid, deep and strong,
Reaching to the root, my life—
What I'd give, to have him back.
Room, dark. Sparks fly,
Fireflies fleeing. Mine.

He whispers while I choke:
"Your uncle would never hurt you."

The last spark dwindles. Dies.

Passing

It's times like this when
your ghost haunts me most:
Halloween with all its trappings.
Sam Spade's wisdom:
the thrill's no good
without the threat of death.
I look everywhere for your ghost,
longing for that shivering touch.
I've locked myself in closets, hoping,
through the hunger and thirst,
the fainting dark,
to taste some trace of you—
if only in passing.

Homecoming

Last night, Dad came by. My sister and I
rushed to meet him at the door, to catch him when he stumbled
getting out of his galoshes. "It's wet out there," he said
mildly, and my brother cried, "You're dead—"
And so it was. I didn't have time to be nice.
"Don't talk about that! Don't mention it! Don't say another word!"
They wanted to protest—argue the morality of silence—
but I leaped over them, back at Dad's side
to smooth his wrinkled brow as we had in the hospital,
smoothing back the few strands of gray hair
upon a dome that had been unnaturally hot and tight,
his skin already hardening like plastic,
red as it always got in summer, as he strained to breathe.

This time, I flung back a look of reproach to ward off their worries,
crouched beside him, murmuring it was all right, I was here—
as I had done then. My sister pumped a red bicycle cylinder
to inflate his lungs. "I don't know how long it'll last,"
she muttered to me, her long, thin fingers as gentle and precise
with the incision in Dad's back that the doctors botched,
as if she was feeding her fledglings, fallen from the nest,
their legs crippled beyond repair, yet still they lived
as she cupped them in her hands, taught them to sing,
fed them, and answered every cry that spoke their zest for life.
Dad woke startled, as he sometimes did
from a sound sleep, so deep we had to shake him,
call "Daddy" in his ear, and he'd jerk suddenly,
call "Whazat?" in a muffled, sleepy voice.

Still caught in his chest, his voice sounded hollow
above the air wheezing out his back.
But this was no zombie. This was Dad,
chuckling deep as we helped him sit up in his crimson shirt,
one of his favorites, and it hid nicely any blood
the hospital or our procedure left behind.
"What did I miss?" he asked me quietly,
as my brothers argued about whether to bring their kids,
and my mother, sister, and sister's boyfriend
greeted him with loud and happy cheers
as if this was his birthday party. I glared at them,
but I didn't dare to comment—it would only draw his attention
to what they did. He was sharp. Sitting there,
hands on his knees like at the doctor's office,
he watched their faces, eyes following one to another
as he puzzled it out. I babbled quickly about a dustup
with a publisher, the *Star Trek* movie we'd planned to see
together (had his ghost sat with me?), remembering how
those other times it was my tears, my gushing, "Daddy,
Daddy, I've missed you, I love you so much!"—
that shocked him into dying again.

He always wakes with amnesia of his death—
perhaps the only way that minds can cope—
is it like this for all the dead? They can't remember the end,
or they'd remember what comes after.
So now I prattle like a child, all the inconsequential things
he's missed, our daily lives, anything
except what I most longed to say back then

while he lay in the hospital, my throat tight
with how much I loved and would miss him,
how much his life made mine,
lest the shock of what I said catapult him into death.
How many more times can his body stand
being reinflated like a bald bicycle tire? How long can I bear
not showing him my elation, my grief?
But I couldn't stand seeing him so bewildered,
in mute sorrow at odds with my fierce, unrepentant joy
at seeing him simply live.

The Halloween Mask

I came downstairs carefully,
holding my tail in one hand,
the railing high above in the other.
Blackness pressed the windows,
dotted with stars—the tiny lights
of a few country neighbors.
My mother waited to bundle me up
for my first Halloween.

In the kitchen, by one dim light,
a giant's head brushed the ceiling.
Familiar creased black pants and green jacket
were topped by a demon's face,
a red snarl full of the fury of the universe,
an anger so alien to my gentle father
I knew this must be some stranger.
I screamed and screamed.

I didn't believe it when
my laughing father pulled off a rubber face,
sockets black and eyeless,
the mask wiggling while he laughed.
At last Dad's face smoothed
of that dangerous laughter,
then gathered wrinkles to show
he understood my worry.
Not until he hid the mask behind his back
and promised not to wear it again
did I recognize
my father-friend.

Calling All Witches

We'll have a witches' bee,
swap lists of great Halloween books
and witch's brew recipes.
A witch in training knows
her best friend is her cat.
An independently-minded witch
balances her checkbook before balancing her spells,
clips coupons and reads recipes first to determine
which ingredients she can afford to buy.
Witching is a calling—like poetry, it demands
determination, dedication, passion, and time—
and an independent income.
Better keep that full-time job.
Recipes for witchery can be found
by looking hard at crafts from your past—
from back in a day when being a witchwife
meant simple know-how and common sense
and home remedies and Women's Arts
like sewing and canny canning,
and an old wives' tale was the very best kind.
Look to the stitchery, the painstaking crochet patterns,
the crewelwork, the hems and seams lined up so perfectly
that corduroy weft and cotton print patterns match on both sides.
Check for your name sewed in the collar
and maybe a little charm or two,
like a sweet tiny bunny made of the same fabric as your front pocket
where it rides, peeking out of your dress:

"Just a little good luck to carry through your day"—
which maybe explains how you found your way safely home
when a careless bus driver
carried his lone remaining shy passenger
way out into the countryside
after her first day of school.

Black Cat Halloween

We Halloween cats—
we know our mission, even if you do not.
We stalk you, shred your cunning disguises with our claws,
rending them to reveal—
not only the monsters you are underneath,
but that the faces you hate,
that you can't stand to look at in the mirror,
are perfectly ordinary.
You'd blend into a crowd.
Your own dark thoughts,
slipping sly as black cats through the night,
their furry black chins piling head upon head,
aren't enough to make you unique.
We're each ourselves, but who can tell
one black cat from another on this wall?
Some just a little fatter, some with stripes
that fade into black, smooth velvet fur, and night itself.
We carry Halloween on our backs,
shred the night with mighty claws
till it tears free of its moorings,
and carry it home.
We drape it over you like a tent,
cutting you off from time and space for a single night:
you can't tell for certain, but you feel it,
that sense you're in another world, another zone.
The blanket sifts softly down about your head,
subtle, sneaky, closer and closer—
you panic as you feel its touch, hair rising,
knowing something's wrong, and near—

but you can still breathe
through the cloth of night,
even if the breath comes faster
through little cat nostrils
shaped like Man Ray's violin
where we've lovingly poked you inside,
nestling deep through f-holes into the bones
of your new cat's body,
stuffing you in soundly
with sharp little claw pricks,
hiding you deep in our
black cat Halloween.

House 5

There's danger I won't live to see the end—
The lights go up, but I'll still sit right there,
My seat propped back, fake butter on my hand,
Loose popcorn on my shirt—but I won't care.
It happened once before. A man's gray hair
Rested so still against the seat. Our bland
Theater tape piped in the latest Cher—
Our lingering patron looked the type to stand,
Shake out his topcoat, tilt his dapper hat,
Pick up his cane and walk out like a king,
And tip the usher who let him out the rear.
We swept up, noisy, wanting him to stir,
Hoping for snore or sneeze, for sudden start
When we scraped dustpans. Was it just his heart?
Perhaps his age was right. But what of Pat,
Our newly minted old-enough-for-R,
A movie buff since ten? Each week he'd bring
A different girl, his wink to us the same.
We liked to walk down during scary parts,
To watch their faces—yes, to hear their screams.
He had a pair of lungs. After, he'd grin
As if it was the best fun in the world,
His arm clamped tight around his shaking girl.
He liked House 5 the best—it was most dim.
We found his curly head against the seat,
His girl hysterical, his eyes alone
Moving in his pallid, stricken face,
No reason—just that seat, where one old man—
He died soon after. Whispered usher lore
Grew dark. House 5 was cold. We feared it then.

We watched while friends within the Box Office tried,
In secret, subtle, at our manager's side,
To steer guests clear and undersell House 5.
It didn't work. No boss likes empty shows,
And some shifts Box was scornful of our fears,
While we had other jobs and school. That's why
We came to work one night and found that hush,
Again—young mother, dead—her baby, too.
Our night-cop watched us all with gimlet eye
And we decided, desperate, what to do.

We get free movies—perk for our low pay.
Before, we'd little time—we worked all shifts
To make ends meet. Now we fill up the rows
On staggered schedules, and Booth botches shows
So patrons leave. We tell them House 5's cursed.
They stay away, and 5 gets colder. Days,
It's not so bad; the back door hangs in bursts
And light streams in while our thin crowd's dispersed.
But theater vests won't keep us warm for good.

View of an Evening Sun

Through it all I catch the glints of gold and green
High window's arc from a sun unseen
Hid beyond the poet's vale:
O thou, gleam forth
For but a little while

Sea of sun and sun of spray
I hunger for thine every ray
Lance through the windows and set my clothes afire
Salt, salt sea—tears for a funeral pyre;
One drop for dole will only take me higher

O little sun of very little room
Arcing to sanctify the distant gloom
Come to me sometime when your sea runs red—
Your bones, tears dyed in murder's rusty spread;
And I will make your screams my featherbed

Salvaging the *Monitor*

The thundering deep. It booms around me,
Hollow, the echo of a hundred years.
This is how flesh is made bone, slipping free in the silt
Like this uniform I no longer need.
This is how eyes become pearls,
Jelly bursting to mingle with the waves,
Till my vision is as wide as the sea.
This is the peace beyond, this drifting tunnel,
This grave of iron with its single tower
Upturned in the deep, soft mud that fills my mouth.
This, what we died for—to lie here guarding her final hour.
Time stretches in our fellowship, in this drifting.
The dead have no need to talk.
Our grave speaks for us: iron monument, first of its kind.
I cannot desert my comrades after so long.
We lie together, commingled bones rocked in our ark
While whale-song arcs, cathedral overhead,
Deep echo down through time.

I hear it first—men's voices, the chop of propellers.
The world of air still holds surprises.
Are these men, wrapped in funereal black,
Umbilical cords stretched out behind,
Dark streamers that tug at a shadow rippling overhead?
They kick straight toward us, as if to do us homage,
Last respects. We never had a service,
Nothing but the ship ablaze and the bells ringing
As we sank, swallowed between one heartbeat and the next.
Long overdue, our rescuers, slick as seals,
Kick toward us through the currents.
Agitating the creatures of the deep
With raucous sawing, they tear free our turret.
We've been at peace too long.

Four Halloween Haiku

Halloween fog glows:
Unearthly green light veils earth,
dresses ghosts dance in

Red moon horizon:
Huge face looms monstrous, leering
Jack-o'-lantern sky

Ghost in my closet
Soft knocks: a lonely night shared
Morse Code with the dead

Without the time waltz
I'm just a painted woman
Chained to her clockwork

Ghost Fleet

The ghost ships glide
Past mist and moon
Unseen, a breath held

The black mirror holds
The spirit ships close
As they slip, standing

Seas for souls
Sharp shadows cut
Fleet air with frost

Lost lives loose
Such patterns traced
Chart hidden lands

Lives, sparkling flakes
Like snow, like motes
in frozen eyes

Slow, sly, we see
Skate patterns traced
In chill sunrise.

Rildix Falls

Rildix falls again, again,
Through the burning night,
With cracks too loud for ear to bear,
With fires that blaze too bright.

The walls resume, then burst anew;
Like mountains pile the dead.
The tongues of fire leap higher, higher,
Till Ash reigns there instead.

Once more the Rildix Great One dies,
Holds tight his final breath,
Clutching his heart in meaty hands
To fend the walls from death.

Once more the Rildix' frenzied chant
Brings corpses to defend;
Once more his slain spread their disease
To foe along with friend.

The madness roars contagiously;
The corpse-breached walls gape wide;
Hysteria tramples through the land
That was the Rildix' pride.

Too late, the son with death-faced force
Sweeps thundering through the street,
And hooves crunch bone as the son alone
Hunts down the Great One's seat.

The Rildix warps in humming death,
Heart clutched in bloodied hands;
And moan-gales shake the portal where
The cold son stiffly stands.

The king lifts ponderous, blood-swelled head;
The blackened, cracked lips part:
The son, for fear of father's curse,
Impales the old man's heart.

The Rildix grins. The heart stands cold,
But dead lips speak at last:
"My bright boy, had you stayed your hand,
Mine anger would have passed."

Through tooth-gapped walls the stiff wind screams;
There are no human calls.
"Now you must die the coward's death
Each time that Rildix falls.

"You rode to save the city, boy?
You sought to ease the dead?
Now you will sup, imbibe their pain,"
Confides the bloody head.

"The city that you scorned to aid,
Whose last defense you slew,
Will rise again eternally
To act this night anew.

"And you must feel each shattered limb,
Pour blood for each blown lung.
You'll beg for death beneath their skulls."
The black lips stutter, done.

The ghost-walls tremble like mirage
Where the Rildix bade them rise;
The corpses, human-featured, sink,
As the Great One's death-chant dies.

But smoldering eyes burst forth once more
Till the young man shouts, in flames:
And scored cheeks nurse that final curse
For the son the Rildix blames.

Now Rildix falls in scarlet fire
Each time this chant is told;
And Rildix repeats itself on earth,
A tragedy far too old.

Can no one stop the Rildix' curse
And end our fearful plight?
For Rildix falls again, again,
All through the burning night.

Morning

Each morning I wake and stare
at the ceiling, our painted spaceship
floating in a sea of stars that dim with dawn.
I'm afraid to look anywhere else.
I fix myself up there, fighting to forget
what makes my heart beat so hard
just to find myself breathing. I can't turn off
the heavy smell—blood and dead meat—but memory, at least,
fails before the sticky mass that damps my sheets,
the source of the tackiness that coats my hands.
I turn my head, then stop at the feel of
short tufts of tawny fur that tickle my arms and cheeks,
hair that's fallen out to coat my pillow like down,
cut off from me as I eased into slumber,
back into the old me. The window's open.
I don't want to know whose knee
I'm clutching like a grisly teddy bear.
The aftertaste of blood is sharp and sweet.
My human self seeks quick similes:
the tang's like orange, some citrus-flavored meat.
I need these lies to hide the deep delight
that causes me to lick my lips,
to pat my matted head, pulling out shreds of heart
still clinging to my regrown human hair—
stuck firmly as lost love. I wish that I were dead.
I lie still, while the blood sings through my limbs
against my will. I don't dare rise.
Each morning I lie still for an hour at least,
fighting the world I wake to, hating
the dawn that brings the room to life.

I can't bring myself to swing my legs and stand.
Already with wakefulness this heavy weight
crushes my chest—the burden of *his* body, limp with death,
the one memory I cannot escape.
I try to hold it in, not to breathe—not to cry.
But he's everywhere, my absent husband,
marked out by the space he left behind—
this cold sheet, this bunched pillow where I bury my nose
for his full-bodied scent—drawing him in so close, so real—
I fling the bedclothes back, run down the hall—
stop, panting, hand pressing my heart
as I see they're safe, two miniature heads intact,
two small bodies shivering with breath.
I take a step toward them, and there he is!
Shining athwart the threshold, my husband's ghost
stands sentinel, his eyes imploring, loving—
warden with a wicked wound clawed out of his chest.
The blood dissipates like smoke when it strikes the floor.
He opens his arms to me, just like that night he saved me.
I couldn't see for hunger. I howled until he opened the door,
then asked him just to check, please check—
said I heard the children crying. When he left to look,
I chewed through the straps.
He blocked the way—one last embrace—
Now I stand watching, tears upon my face,
as his ghost smiles that everything's all right—
once more, our daughters made it through the night.

Ghost

Grandma's
House is alive.
Our visit's full—Grandpa's
Spirit, her past. Gone, she's still here,
Talking.

Waking Beauty

The time they lose is not the same as mine.
No spell decreed they'd not decay with time
Like cheese and cherries, chocolate, even wine
That blackens to a sludge, drips free in slime—
No life but mold within this cage of mine.

Our clothes thinned out with heat, with cold, with rain,
Till wind cleared final threads to clean my frame.
Friends, family crumble round me, long past pain
(I weep in dreams but slumber just the same)—
My family rots—statues of dust remain.

He sneaks in, spooked to see he's not alone—
But gray protectors' shadowed eyes can't roam.
He chuckles, knocks off heads, climbs on the throne
While gray dust flurries, falls on me like foam.
He sees me naked—I can't even groan.

He seals it with a kiss. I wake to spleen:
All that I've suffered bursts out in a scream:
The fairy, family, princeling libertine—
I throw him off and brain him with a beam.
The worst is I'm awake—alone—the queen.

My family's dead, land ravaged—queen of none.
They'd live in dreams, but anxious sleep won't come—
Or brings slow deaths and prince's cruel fun.
Insomniac, slept up a lifetime's sum,
I'm trapped in waking nightmares. Evil's won.

Godolin's Remains

In the evening, in the chamber
Of the far Millashian lord,
Scent of incense, char of umber
Wafted roofward with a Word,
A mystic rune—a seer with vision,
Speaking unto Rala's thanes:
"We need someone for a mission:
Seek out Godolin's remains."

"We need some warrior for this challenge,
One with mind of fire and steel,
One with skill enough to unhinge
The illusion from the real,"
Spoke Rala Millash, son of Harmon,
Unto those that graced his hall,
The archers and the warrior women:
"Find the false Arimishal!"

Then rose the Queen from seat of honor,
Stepped into the Mystic's Place:
"O warriors, you have heard the wonder
Of Arimishal's fall from grace.
He it was who called the thunder
To do battle with our swords:
It shattered halls and blades asunder;
Stopped up all the Mystic's words.

"And I have seen, within my Tower,
Sights to make the stout heart weep:
Arimishal, that jealous hoarder,
Gathers power in his Keep:
He sacrifices maids and young men,
Steals their life-force for his aims;
I know of but one way to stop him:
Seek out Godolin's remains!"

Now upspoke the aged Mystic,
Laid his hand upon his staff:
"When the seers first gathered, struck
By horror, and from there to wrath,
By the gruesome deeds he plotted,
We Mystics laid on him a curse;
But fighting off the pall, he hid:
His counter-spells left us the worse.

"He draws more power to him daily
By a lost and arcane means
That none here have strength to fight but
Godolin, of other times.
Just one thing we know to stop him
Out of all curses and banes;
Since long dead is Godolin,
Seek out Godolin's remains!"

Under the tall and smoky rafters
Rose three fighters, lank and grim—
"Yasha, Lestor, and Aeorthas,"
Spoke Aeorthas for her kin,
"Will do this thing: upon the Hair
Of the Goddesses Lohs and Zäl,
We'll seek out and retrieve, we swear,
The bane of foul Arimishal."

The Queen accepted, and the warriors
Journeyed long under the moon;
Fought through moor and crashed through forest,
Conquered the mountain Râl, and soon
Entered the land of Orphalestés,
Where Mage Godolin once dwelt;
Banished ghosts, discerned false graves,
Until beside his own they knelt.

Cautiously they dug by oak till
They had pulled forth ancient bones;
They stuffed these in a sack, and took all
That remained within the ruins.
Then back to Rala's hall they carried
Godolin's bones, and eyes, and hood;
The Mystics gathered, gaunt and wearied
From battling Arimishal's horde.

While many watched, the Mystics fashioned
A spell out of the ancient days;
With Godolin's remains they formed
A thing Arimishal could not slay.
It held the Words of Power once
Bespoke by Godolin the seer;
They raised him from his sleep of silence,
Sent him to find Arimishal's lair.

Arimishal took one step backward,
Trying to outreach his foe;
He hurled a lightning runespell forward,
But that curse was much too slow.
Godolin spoke. A scream of horror
At the Mage raised from the dead:
Arimishal, for all his power,
Fell before Godolin's hood.

But even as they feasted, victors,
In that far Millashian hall—
Mystics, Yasha, Lestor, Aeorthas—
Forth there rang a hollow call.
From beyond the walls it sounded,
Echoing beneath the sky:
"Though I have lain by oak wood bounden,
I will reckon: you shall die!"

At first the Mystics laughed, uncertain;
But fearful grew their bleary gaze.
Within the hour they stank of gangrene,
And the torn land, bandits seized.
Those not killed by plague or poison
Fell by sword, fire, or worse pain;
Demolished lies the land of those who
Dared touch Godolin's remains.

Starkness

The sky is desolate and dark gray-blue;
The wind gusts intermittently, speaking of rain—
The which I feel will never come—dry rain.
My peace, gone in an instant, torn from me
By those grim, silent clouds which smudge like doom.
A blackbird suddenly appears from nowhere,
Flies over my head and alights on a smooth gray tree,
Cocking his head with a too-knowing stare;
And up ahead, four and twenty of them
Storm into the air.

Halloween's Expiration

Wild November wind
Trees lash. Autumnal fury
Howls grief's raging breath

Breath whines through his throat
My black cat's season too short
Cuts my raging heart

Witches We

The moon shone so brightly on the dark lake,
a ladder of moonlight stretched like pearls on black velvet,
connecting us to heaven. Despite the cool evening,
it didn't take much persuading:
"Let's go for a dip," I suggested, "just us two witches together,"
and my sister ran up into the boathouse
to change and turn on a homing beacon
so we could distinguish our shore from all the other night-clad cottages
that merged into the impenetrable woods in the darkness.
One, two, three: we jumped in, transforming
the painful shock of the cold lake
into whoops of triumph. "Yes!
It feels icy now, but just wait until I try that new popsicle spell!"

Witches together, we bobbed in the night surf of Keuka Lake
while small, beautiful bats darted overhead with tiny cheeps,
and my sister's little gray tuxedo cat watched worriedly from the windows,
waiting to see if we dissolved into the midnight waves
and melted clean away.
We had the whole lake for our cauldron,
with the moon already inside.
We named the living ingredients:
my friend the large catfish who ruled the fish in these parts
with a generous twitch of black moustaches;
our Dad's chortle of glee as he emerged from his soaring swan dive
every summer, now many summers past (the lake remembers);
the small, slatey stones on which I'd drawn messages every summer
before skipping them out as far as they would go,
carrying words like wishes.

Not even my sister knew what those messages contained.
Only the lake knew—and my fishy friends,
reading curiously as the stones sank into the soppy mud of the lake's floor,
stirring up a small green-brown explosion.

Layers and layers of Keuka memories stitched across both our lives,
with this lake running deep as the heart through us both.
We swam up the moon's ladder, two witches together,
a secret meeting, talking of witchy things:
our shared love of Ruth Chew, who awakened magic in us both
with her children's books *The Wednesday Witch* and *What the Witch Left*,
stories to which I'd introduced my sister when she was only four,
and I, at nine, feeling so worldly-wise, a grown-up witch
who swam with her magical fish-finding rock every summer
and sought out secret, magical clues in every Halloween party.
My sister had taken it one step farther:
after we'd plumbed the secrets of Mom's dresser drawers,
seeking magical treasures like Ruth Chew's heroines,
my sister struck up quite a correspondence with the author,
until at last the greatest witch we knew
had written one last time to say
she couldn't exchange any more letters due to a severe lack of time.
She drew a picture of a witch crying,
prompting my sister to write even more,
generously donating her own time
to replace the time Ruth had lost.

As grown witches now, we knew enough
to make our own magic. We found it everywhere:
the marvel of a double rainbow;
the loyal black cat who rode my shoulders and snuggled close
to guard me by night with his predecessor's kind green eyes;
the miracle of loved ones visiting in dreams.
In the beautiful solitude of Keuka Lake at night
we sank into the lights reflecting from the farther shore like colored lanterns:
blue, green, red, white, yellow,
and the moon so high above, as far as a castle wall—
a celestial castle closing its gates
in a massive wall of clouds
lined cobalt and silver-gray like armor,
while the moon shone through an open casement,
illuminating the distant shore
like the painting of a shipwreck come to life:
that high drama, a lighting so striking none could believe
except we who had seen it,
the moon opening her vault of magic to us high up in the sky.
We drank in her wisdom with the lake,
ducking down, big gulps of molten silver as soft as snow,
moonlight sprinkling a field of lilies in the black lake's reflected sky.

When we got too tired to swim to shore
after all our back-floating, star-gazing, and magic-working,
our magical cats climbed onto the prow of our old rowboat,
sitting beside the guiding lanterns
while the boat magically rowed to find us,
oars tended by the ghost men that we played baseball with all summer
on the hill above Dad's Field at the entrance to the magical wooded kingdom
beside our childhood home in Keuka Park.
We hung on the handles at the stern, pulled behind the boat,
gliding through black water soft as silk, invisible in the quiet wake,
luxuriating like ghosts.
Anyone looking on would only see
one cat on the prow, one cat on the stern, perched like icons of Bast,
while our chuckles rose invisibly from behind the boat,
an unearthly humor like the voice of Lake Keuka herself.

Many Haunted Returns

New house this year, and we don't know these streets,
though gardens, saltbox houses, and high trees
remind of cottages and country leaves,
our upstate New York home. My nephew, niece,
with trust, excitement, trip ahead to beat
on doors marked grim with skulls and pumpkins, treats
less sought than chances to impart belief
in alter-ego-heroes, our brave feats.
"I'll save you!" echoes through the dark to meet
lost whimpers in the maze of dead-end streets.

Die Alone, the Demon Said

Do I have to die?
I'm very small. I won't
Eat anything at all.

Alone's all right, if you'll come too.
Let's crunch some bones. I'm ready to.
Or let's read Poe till lights grow dim—chill
Nights we let the raven in.
Enter terror, dusk, and dark.

The bed is cold. I don't miss Clark.
He chose to leave. I couldn't hold—
Evil loves no heart of gold.

Demons chew my entrails tart—
Eventually I'll love this part.
My anguish grows, a separate beast—
One for the head, and one to feast—
No saints without the torment first—

So come and help me! Do your worst!
At least I'll know I was your first—
Is death not love—my Self to kill?
Delicious demon, do your will.

About Your Haunted Host

Adele Gardner—

Urges you to visit the Poe Museum in Richmond, Virginia. Complete with black cats Edgar and Pluto! www.poemuseum.org/poe-museum-cats

Dove into their parents' unabridged Poe collection at age eleven, thanks to the incomparable Vincent Price.

Served as curator of the *SFPA 2019 Halloween Poetry Reading,* Science Fiction & Fantasy Poetry Association, www.sfpoetry.com/hw/19halloween.html

Fell in love with *The Halloween Tree* by Ray Bradbury at twelve. Traveled across the country to meet Ray Bradbury twelve years later; he signed this favorite with a drawing of a Jack-o'-Lantern!

Learned to machine-sew at thirteen specifically to make Halloween costumes (home-assembled since age seven). Favorites include: a black cat, Mr. Spock, Uncle Dan, Lenore from "The Raven," Commissioner Gordon, the Doctor (Who?), Princess and Jason from *Battle of the Planets,* Cheetara from *ThunderCats,* and the fabled "Miss Paper" (intended to be the Tin Woodsman, but what kid wants to argue with an award for Most Original Costume?). Also Hamlet. And Gandalf. And the narrator of Poe's "Berenice," complete with teeth.

First created a Halloween book (sadly, no longer extant) at age six. Niece and nephew Kaitlyn and Adam carried on this tradition, gifting Adele with handmade Halloween books (a true treasure).

Wrote their first poems on Halloween themes. Has poems and stories in many Halloween tomes. Proud member of the Horror Writers Association, Science Fiction & Fantasy Poetry Association, and Poetry Society of Virginia.

Often creates Halloween stories and poems by night on black paper with silver ink, or with a quill pen . . . with a toy raven nearby . . . a living black cat . . . and, hopefully, some ghosts.

Designed haunted houses for the Gardner family starting at age nine, for which Mom gamely took on many spooky roles. As an adult, Adele performed nested

costume changes from a witch to the Phantom of the Opera to a skeleton . . .
frightening the kids a little too much!

Frequents local Halloween & Poe attractions. A small sampling: Edgar Allan Poe
at Fort Eustis; Haunted Hampton Tours (Hampton History Museum, including
Edgar Allan Poe); Howl-o-Scream (Busch Gardens Williamsburg); Haunted Horse
Rides at the Hampton Carousel; Poe-themed Unhappy Hour at the Casemate
Museum; many haunted farms, trails, historic houses, parks and ballparks, including
a hunt for the Witch of Pungo in Virginia Beach (one of the scariest!); The Big
Read: *Great Tales and Poems* by Edgar Allan Poe, Virginia Beach Public Library
System; and many more. Poe Museum!

Adele is literary executor for beloved father, mentor, and namesake Delbert R.
Gardner.

ADELE GARDNER (gardnercastle.com, none/they/Mx.) is a fiction writer
& award-winning poet with over 475 stories and poems in *Analog Science Fiction
and Fact, Clarkesworld, Strange Horizons, PodCastle, Daily Science Fiction,* and more.
A graduate of the Clarion West Writers Workshop, this genderfluid night owl
loves libraries, samurai films, and reading comics with cats. Adele co-chaired the
2022 Dwarf Stars Award with Greer Woodward: sfpoetry.com/ds/22dwarfstars.html

To hear the author read "Halloween Hearts" and a few other
poems from this collection, check out Adele's appearance in the
Speculative Sundays Poetry Reading Series hosted by Akua Lezli Hope:
www.facebook.com/watch/live/?ref=watch_permalink&v=424716092501347

Acknowledgements

"Golden Eye," "Halloween's Expiration," "Halloween Hearts," "The Halloween Mask," "Many Haunted Returns," and "Pandemic Food Delivery" are original to this collection.

I am so grateful to the following for publishing and honoring my work. (Some appeared under prior bylines C. A. Gardner, Lyn C. A. Gardner, Carolyn A. Gardner, etc.)

"Black Cat Halloween," Third Place, Casablanca Memorial Award of the Poetry Society of Virginia, May 24, 2019. *Poetry Virginia 2019: Collected Poems from the Poetry Society of Virginia*, Ed. Jeff Hewitt, Feb. 1, 2020.

"Black Cat Spare," *Eternal Haunted Summer*, Autumn Equinox 2014, Sept. 22, 2014.

"Calling All Witches," *Spectral Realms*, No. 13, Summer 2020.

"The Catty Hours," Honorable Mention, Balticon Poetry Contest, May 2021. Published in the convention souvenir book, the *BSFAN*, BSFS (Baltimore Science Fiction Society), May 2021.

"The Chant of the Black Cats," *Jack-o'-Spec: Tales of Halloween and Fantasy*, Ed. Karen A. Romanko, Raven Electrick Ink, 2011. Reprinted, *The 2012 Rhysling Anthology: The Best Science Fiction, Fantasy, and Horror Poetry of 2011*, selected by members of the Science Fiction & Fantasy Poetry Association, Ed. Lyn C. A. Gardner, Science Fiction & Fantasy Poetry Association, 2012. Nominated in the long poem category for the Rhysling Award. Audio read by the author, *SFPA 2016 Halloween Poetry Reading*, curated by Stace Johnson, Science Fiction & Fantasy Poetry Association, Oct. 2016.

"The Cost," *Dreaming of Days in Astophel* by Lyn C. A. Gardner, Sam's Dot Publishing, 2011.

"Die Alone, the Demon Said," *Tales of the Talisman*, Vol. 9, Iss. 3, Winter 2013/14. Included as Featured Poet in *Disturbed Digest: Dark Fantasy and Horror*, #17, June 2017, 5th Anniversary Double Issue.

"Eureka," *Mythic Delirium* 24, Winter/Spring 2011. Reprinted, *Dark Metre*, Iss. 18, Jan. 6, 2013.

Four Halloween Haiku:
"Ghost in my closet," *Scifaikuest: A Magazine of Minimalist Poetry*, Nov. 2011, print ed., Vol. IX, No. 2. Reprinted, *Halloween Haiku II and Other Hauntings*, Ed. Lester Smith, Popcorn Press, 2014. "Halloween fog glows," "Red moon horizon," and "Without the time waltz," *Halloween Haiku*, Ed. Lester Smith, Popcorn Press, 2011.

"Ghost," *Halloween Haiku II and Other Hauntings*, Ed. Lester Smith, Popcorn Press, 2014.

"Ghost Fleet," *Whispering Spirits Digital Magazine*, No. 19, Iss. 2, Nov. 2008.

"Godolin's Remains," *Contemporary Rhyme*, Vol. 3, No. 2, Spring 2006. Reprinted, *The Hungry Dead*, Ed. Lester Smith, Popcorn Press, Dec. 2010. Included as Featured Poet in *Disturbed Digest: Dark Fantasy and Horror*, #17, June 2017, 5th Anniversary Double Issue.

"Gone the Sun," *Tapestry*, Iss. 9 & 10, April 2006.

"Haunt Me," *Mythic Delirium*, Iss. 3.4, Apr.-June 2017.

"Home," *Mythic Delirium*, Iss. 26, Winter/Spring 2012.

"Home Inspection," *HWA Poetry Showcase*, Vol. VI, Ed. Stephanie M. Wytovich, Horror Writers Association, Nov. 2019.

"Homecoming," *MindFlights*, Halloween issue, Oct. 30, 2010. Reprinted, *The 2011 Rhysling Anthology: The Best SF, Fantasy, and Horror Poetry of 2010*, Ed. David Lunde, SFPA in cooperation with Raven Electrick Ink, 2011. Nominated in the long poem category for the Rhysling Award. Audio read by the author, *SFPA 2013 Halloween Poetry Reading*, Ed. Liz Bennefeld, Science Fiction & Fantasy Poetry Association, Oct. 2013.

"House 5," *Cinema Spec: Tales of Hollywood and Fantasy*, Ed. Karen A. Romanko, Raven Electrick Ink, 2009. Audio read by the author, *SFPA 2010 Halloween Poetry Reading*, Ed. Liz Bennefeld, Science Fiction & Fantasy Poetry Association, Oct. 2010. Reprinted, *Niteblade* #26: A Fixer-Upper, a special ghostly issue of *Niteblade Fantasy and Horror Magazine*, Vol. 26, Dec. 2013.

"I Wander in the Mists," *Sonnet Writers*, Vol. 1, 2006 (published online Dec. 13, 2006, and in print Oct. 2007). Honorable Mention, Flashes of Darkness/Mirrormask Competition, *Future Fire: Speculative Fiction and Dark Fantasy*, Dec. 2005.

"A Keepsake Box for Poe," *Penumbra*, Oct. 2012, Vol. II, Iss. I, Edgar Allan Poe issue. Included as Featured Poet in *Disturbed Digest: Dark Fantasy and Horror*, #17, June 2017, 5th Anniversary Double Issue.

"Late," *Raven Poetrick*, a publication of *Raven Electrick: Tales of Fantasy, Science Fiction, Horror and Mystery*, Halloween Contest Issue (Runner-Up), October 2001. Reprinted, *The Hungry Dead*, Ed. Lester Smith, Popcorn Press, Dec. 2010. Audio read by the author, *SFPA 2006 Halloween Poetry Reading*, Ed. Liz Bennefeld, Science Fiction & Fantasy Poetry Association, Oct. 2006.

"Lenore to Her Tragic Muse, Edgar Allan Poe," *Spectral Realms*, No. 16, Winter 2022.

"Midnight Posture," *Mythic Delirium*, Iss. 23, Summer/Fall 2010. Reprinted, *The 2011 Rhysling Anthology: The Best SF, Fantasy, and Horror Poetry of 2010*, Ed. David Lunde, Science Fiction & Fantasy Poetry Association in cooperation with Raven Electrick Ink, 2011. Nominated in the short poem category for the Rhysling Award.

"Morning," *Death Rattle: A Magazine of Dark Fiction*, Iss. 1, Fall 2010, Halloween issue, Evil Cat Press. Reprinted, *Lupine Lunes: Horror Poems & Short Stories*, Ed. Lester Smith, Popcorn Press, 2016.

"My Little Vampire," *Dreams & Nightmares* 110, Sept. 2018. Reprinted, *The 2019 Rhysling Anthology: The Best Science Fiction, Fantasy & Horror Poetry of 2018*, Ed. David C. Kopaska-Merkel, Science Fiction & Fantasy Poetry Association, 2019. Nominated in the short poem category for the Rhysling Award.

"Nevermore," *Spectral Realms*, No. 13, Summer 2020.

"Our Lady of Darkness," *Wicked Hollow*, Iss. 2, April 2002. Audio read by the author, *SFPA 2007 Halloween Poetry Reading*, Ed. Liz Bennefeld, Science Fiction & Fantasy Poetry Association, Oct. 2007.

"Our Last Halloween," *Spectral Realms*, No. 16, Winter 2022.

"Passing," *Halloween Haiku*, Ed. Lester Smith, Popcorn Press, 2011.

"The Perfect Match," *Sonnet Writers*, Vol. 1, 2006 (published online Dec. 13, 2006, and in print Oct. 2007). Reprinted, *Fickle Muses: An Online Journal of Myth and Legend*, July 7, 2013.

"Poe's Prophets," *Star*Line*, Spring 2014, Vol. 37, Issue 2.

"Reynardine," *Corvid Queen*, Jan. 31, 2020, Folklore category.

"Rildix Falls," *Contemporary Rhyme*, Vol. 2, No. 1, Winter 2005. Reprinted, *The 2006 Rhysling Anthology: The Best SF, Fantasy and Horror Poetry of 2005*, Ed. Drew Morse. Nominated in the long poem category for the Rhysling Award. Reprinted, *The Hungry Dead*, Ed. Lester Smith, Popcorn Press, Dec. 2010. Audio read by the author, *SFPA 2009 Halloween Poetry Reading*, Ed. Liz Bennefeld, Science Fiction & Fantasy Poetry Association, Oct. 2009.

"Salvaging the *Monitor*," *Cider Press Review*, Vol. 8, 2007. Reprinted, *The Hungry Dead*, Ed. Lester Smith, Popcorn Press, Dec. 2010. Audio read by Diane Severson on *Poetry Planet*, No. 4, "Coming Home," *StarShipSofa*, Episode No. 208, Oct. 19, 2011.

"Seven Steps to Reach Your Father across the Great Divide," *Liminality: A Magazine of Speculative Poetry*, Iss. 25, Autumn 2020. Reprinted, *The 2021 Rhysling Anthology: The Best Science Fiction, Fantasy & Horror Poetry of 2020*, Ed. Alessandro Manzetti, Science Fiction & Fantasy Poetry Association, 2021. Nominated in the long poem category for the Rhysling Award.

"Starkness," *Currents*, 1990-91.

"A Tasty Treat," *Spectral Realms*, No. 12, Winter 2020.

"Throat," *Down in the Cellar*, Iss. 6, Winter 2007-08 (published Dec. 2007). Reprinted, *The Hungry Dead*, Ed. Lester Smith, Popcorn Press, Dec. 2010.

"To Hear You Speak," *Dreaming of Days in Astophel* by Lyn C. A. Gardner, Sam's Dot Publishing, 2011.

"View of an Evening Sun," *Hadrosaur Tales*, Vol. 9, 2000.

"Waking Beauty," *Cabinet des Fees: A Journal of Fairy Tales, Scheherezade's Bequest*, Iss. 9, Jan. 2010. Audio read by the author, *SFPA 2011 Halloween Poetry Reading*, Ed. Liz Bennefeld, Science Fiction & Fantasy Poetry Association, Oct. 2011.

"The Witch Girl," *Goblin Fruit*, Autumn 2011, with audio read by the author. Reprinted, *The 2012 Rhysling Anthology: The Best Science Fiction, Fantasy, and Horror Poetry of 2011*, selected by members of the Science Fiction & Fantasy Poetry Association, Ed. Lyn C. A. Gardner, Science Fiction & Fantasy Poetry Association, 2012. Nominated in the long poem category for the Rhysling Award. Audio read by the author, *SFPA 2015 Halloween Poetry Reading*, Ed. Liz Bennefeld and Shannon Connor Winward, Science Fiction & Fantasy Poetry Association, Oct. 2015.

"Witch Habiliments," *Illumen*, Autumn 2012. Audio read by the author, *SFPA 2017 Halloween Poetry Reading*, Ed. Ashley Dioses, Science Fiction & Fantasy Poetry Association, Oct. 2017.

"Witches We," *Bluff & Vine: A Literary Review*, Issue 3, October 2019. Reprinted, *The 2020 Rhysling Anthology: The Best Science Fiction, Fantasy & Horror Poetry of 2019*, Ed. David C. Kopaska-Merkel, Science Fiction & Fantasy Poetry Association, 2020. Nominated in the long poem category for the Rhysling Award.

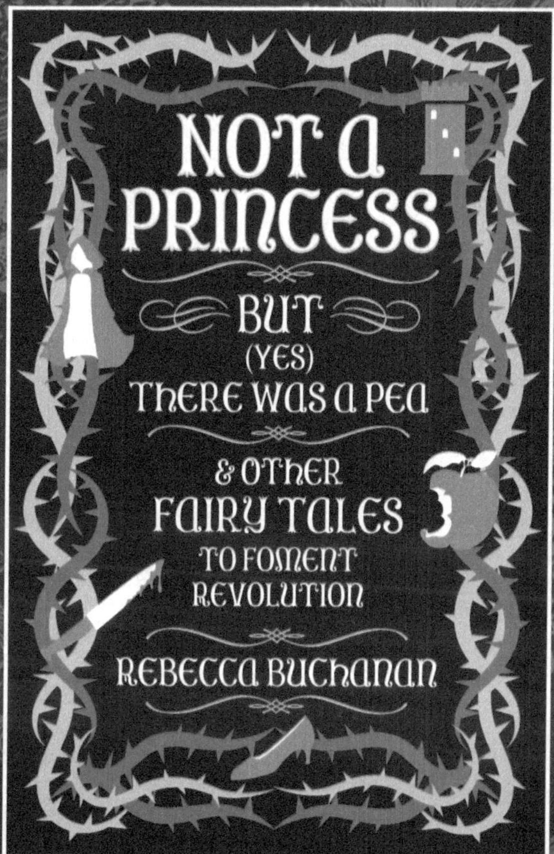

NOT A PRINCESS
BUT
(YES)
THERE WAS A PEA
& OTHER
FAIRY TALES
TO FOMENT
REVOLUTION
REBECCA BUCHANAN

www.ingramcontent.com/pod-product-compliance
Lightning Source LLC
Chambersburg PA
CBHW030805190726
48285CB00003B/1033